Posy patterns

A first book of shapes

Written by Tim Healey
Illustrated by Jo Burroughes

PUBLISHED BY THE READER'S DIGEST ASSOCIATION LIMITED
IN CONJUNCTION WITH mothercare LIMITED

Posy was a little girl who liked making patterns. Sometimes she put all her toys in a straight line with Tina, her favourite, in the middle.

Sometimes she would line up her toys one behind the other with Tina at the front.

When Posy built a tower, Tina went on top.

Posy was always very neat and tidy, but she did have one problem. And the problem's name was Gus.

Gus was her little brother and he was *not* very interested in neat patterns. He spent a lot of time pretending to be an aeroplane.

Sometimes, he might bump into
a line of toys, or knock down a
tower. Then Posy called him
"little pest!"
What on earth was the point of
little brothers?

Posy's mother usually brought
Gus along when she took Posy to
nursery school.
One morning Posy walked all the
way there without treading on a
single crack in the pavement.
She just walked on the squares.

At the nursery there was a draughtboard. Posy did not know how to play the game but she liked to walk her fingers across the squares as if they were paving stones. She took care not to tread on any lines.

The teacher, Carol, helped Posy
to do some printing with poster
paints. First they took
half an onion and
dipped it in paint.
It made a pattern
of circles.

Then they took half an apple
and dipped it in paint. Posy was
surprised. It made the shape
of a star.

Then they carved shapes in half
potatoes and printed them too.
They made the shapes of a cross,
and a diamond, and a triangle,
and a heart.

When her mother came to collect
Posy, Gus found the place where
the paint pots were stacked. He
tipped one of the pots onto the
floor.

Gus dipped his finger in the pool
of paint and tried to draw a
straight line on the wall.

But it came out sort of wriggly.

Then he did a zigzag.

Gus got covered with paint.

He made handprints on the wall . . .

. . . and footprints on the floor.
"Gus!" shrieked his mother.
"Gus!" shouted Posy. "You little
pest!"

"You'll need a good bath when you get home," said his mother, doing her best to wipe off the paint.

On the way home they stopped
at a supermarket. There was a
neat stack of soup tins piled up in
a pyramid.

"Gus! No!"

While Posy and her mother piled
the tins up again, Gus found a
tube of toothpaste.

It was wonderful toothpaste.
With stripes in it!

"Gus! No!"

Posy and her mother were glad
to get out of the shop without any
more disasters.

Back at home Gus was given a good hot bath, and Posy was left in peace. She invented a new game. First she made a circle with mats and cushions on the floor.

Then she jumped from one to another as if they were stepping stones.

It was a brilliant game, but there was just one problem. And the problem's name was Gus.

He kicked up her cushions and
Posy called him "little pest!"
Gus threw a cushion at her. Posy
threw one back.

They had a great fight and by the end of it Posy's pattern was completely ruined.

Their mother came in and made
them tidy the room up.
Then Gus lay on the floor and
watched television while Posy
did a jigsaw.

The picture had a ballerina just
like Tina in it.

Posy filled in the pieces until there was just one left to do. It was the piece with the ballerina's star on it. But where was it?

It was not on the table.

It was not in
the jigsaw box.

Posy looked
all around
but couldn't
see it
anywhere.

It had fallen off the table and
under the sofa. Only one pair of
eyes was low enough to see it.

"There it is!" cried Gus. He
wriggled his arm to reach it.

Then, very proudly, he handed
it over.

Perhaps, thought Posy, there *was*
some point in little brothers
after all . . .

. . . even little brothers . . .

... like Gus!

MY WONDERFUL WORDBOX

First Edition Copyright © 1989
The Reader's Digest Association Limited,
25 Berkeley Square, London W1X 6AB

READER'S DIGEST and The Digest
are registered trademarks of
The Reader's Digest Association, Inc.
of Pleasantville, New York, U.S.A.

mothercare® is the registered
trademark of Mothercare Limited,
Watford, Herts, England

Printed in Hong Kong
16-040-1